Samuel French Acting Edition

Taking Stock

by Richard Schotter

SAMUELFRENCH.COM   SAMUELFRENCH.CO.UK

FOR PRODUCTION ENQUIRIES

UNITED STATES AND CANADA
Info@SamuelFrench.com
1-866-598-8449

UNITED KINGDOM AND EUROPE
Plays@SamuelFrench.co.uk
020-7255-4302

Each title is subject to availability from Samuel French, depending upon country of performance. Please be aware that *TAKING STOCK* may not be licensed by Samuel French in your territory. Professional and amateur producers should contact the nearest Samuel French office or licensing partner to verify availability.

MUSIC USE NOTE

Licensees are solely responsible for obtaining formal written permission from copyright owners to use copyrighted music in the performance of this play and are strongly cautioned to do so. If no such permission is obtained by the licensee, then the licensee must use only original music that the licensee owns and controls. Licensees are solely responsible and liable for all music clearances and shall indemnify the copyright owners of the play(s) and their licensing agent, Samuel French, against any costs, expenses, losses and liabilities arising from the use of music by licensees. Please contact the appropriate music licensing authority in your territory for the rights to any incidental music.

IMPORTANT BILLING AND CREDIT REQUIREMENTS

If you have obtained performance rights to this title, please refer to your licensing agreement for important billing and credit requirements.

This play is dedicated to
Roni and to Marilyn.

Taking Stock was first presented at the Jewish Repertory Theatre, New York from December 29, 1990 to January 27, 1991, directed by Marilyn Chris, with the following cast:

SAM BAKER.........................George Guidall
ALVI STONE............................Lee Wallace
HOWIE GOLDEN ....Stephen Singer

Sets by Ray Recht
Costumes by Gail Cooper-Hecht
Lighting by Najla Hanson
Music by Ronnie Breines
Production Stage Manager: Nina Heller
Casting by Stephanie Klapper

CHARACTERS

ALVI STONE, a man around sixty

SAM BAKER, a man around sixty

HOWIE GOLDEN, a man in his thirties

SETTING

Sam and Alvi's Sporting Goods, Upper West Side, Manhattan.

TIME

The Present.

ACT I

Monday morning. Late May.

ACT II

One week later.

ACT I

LIGHTS low. The setting is a sporting goods-store. It's the kind of place that was in its hey-day in the nineteen-fifties. Run-down, cluttered, filled with athletic equipment of all kinds—baseball gloves, bats, football helmets, etc. There is a counter stage right with a stool on either side. On the counter is a cash register, adding machine, ledger books. Stage left, three connected chairs and a stool for trying on sneakers. Stage center is a display carousel with jerseys, shirts, etc. It is late May. Suffused light. The LIGHTS rise dim and we see the figure of a man around sixty, doing deep-knee bends. HE wears a baseball cap and groans loudly after each knee bend. HE continues a few moments and another MAN appears. Also around sixty. HE wears a fancy running suit, has Walkman earphones on his head and carries magazines and a brown paper bag. IIE watches the exercising figure a few moments from the door.

SAM. Alvi? Is that you?

ALVI. Yeah. It's me. Who'd you think it was?

SAM. I didn't know. I couldn't see you in the dark. (*HE flips on light switch. LIGHTS come up full. SAM moves to connected chairs stage left, sits down, opens bag, takes out a container of coffee and two danish pastries. ALVI does another knee bend.)* Doing exercises, huh?

ALVI. What does it look like I'm doing?

SAM. Just asking.

ALVI. Why do you always ask what I'm doing when you can see perfectly well I'm doing it?

SAM. It's how I make conversation. I ask questions.

ALVI. For forty years, all I've heard from you are questions. Just one morning I'd like you to walk in here, hang up your coat, put your bag on the counter and be quiet.

SAM. You're in a lousy mood this morning.

ALVI. That's right. So keep out of my way.

SAM. I don't see how anyone could be in a lousy mood on a morning like this. It's beautiful out there. You know what I did this morning? Ran in the park. Two miles. Right around the reservoir. That's the way to start the day. Sun heating up your shoulders. Lungs breathing hard. Legs pumping up and down beneath you. Makes you know you're alive. Maybe if you ran in the morning, you wouldn't be in such a lousy mood.

ALVI. My mood's got nothing to do with running.

SAM. What's it got to do with?

ALVI. I don't like emergency inventories. Especially after the Memorial Day sale. *(ALVI stops exercising, goes behind counter and takes out ledger books.)*

SAM. I like it like this. Peaceful. Quiet. Just you and me. Like the old days. Doing inventory. Shooting the breeze. Taking stock.

ALVI. I just checked the books. We're down ten percent. Height of the season, and we're down ten percent! (*Pause.*) Know what this means?

SAM. It means we do inventory. Next month we're up, and everything's fine.

ALVI. It's not going to be fine. Howie Golden's coming over this morning to tell us how high he's raising the rent. Millie's Lingerie just went out. You know that?

SAM. No.

ALVI. After thirty years, he raises her four hundred percent. The same thing could happen to us. (*Pause.*) Remember how Millie took care of old lady Golden? Hours she spent with her. Fitting her with corsets, bras, undergarments of every description. She gave her personal attention, Sammy. No question too small to answer. In those days, there was such a thing as courtesy. As graciousness. As service. (*Pause. Notices Sam's jogging sui*t.) What's that get-up you're wearing?

SAM. The Super Jogger's suit. Came in yesterday. Like it?

ALVI. You look ridiculous.

SAM. I thought I looked snappy.

ALVI. You used to wear a Mets T-shirt and a pair of baggy pants and you looked fine. These days, I don't even know who you are.

SAM. I'm keeping up with the times.

ALVI. I'm not paying for Super Jogger suits so you can keep up with the times.

SAM. I paid for it. Don't worry.

ALVI. If I don't worry, who will?

SAM. What's that supposed to mean?

ALVI. It means I worry about higher rents while you prance around in Super Jogger suits.

SAM. I worry too.

ALVI. All you worry about these days is night school and tennis games. We're not here for our health, Sammy. We have to take inventory and then prepare for the worst. (*ALVI begins looking over ledger books.*)

SAM. (*Pause.*) What do you think he'll raise us?

ALVI. Who can tell? The way I figure, if we cut corners, maybe we could handle twenty-four hundred a month. That's a hundred percent increase. If he asks for more, it's time to pack our bags.

SAM. He won't ask for more. We go back so many years with his old man. He grew up in this store.

ALVI. You think he cares about that? No way. He's like the rest of the snotnoses these days. He cares about the bottom line and nothing more. (*Pause. Looks at watch.*) Christ, Sammy. It's nine-thirty. He'll be here any minute. Let's start counting.

SAM. I can't.

ALVI. Why not?

SAM. I'm not comfortable. A person has to be comfortable when he works or his efficiency declines. I read that in *Psychology Today,* March issue.

ALVI. What's going to make you comfortable?

SAM. How about a little morning chatter?

ALVI. You want morning chatter, turn on talk radio. Today, we take stock. The usual way. I shout, you answer, I write.

SAM. I have to limber up first.

ALVI. (*Irritated.*) Go ahead. Limber up. But make it snappy.

(SAM goes into a yoga position, puts his head between his legs and begins to chant.)

ALVI. What kind of limbering up is that?

SAM. Yoga. It's incredible what five minutes like this does for you. The blood rushes to your head, you get oxygenized, and you're ready to go.

ALVI. Get up from there and start counting.

SAM. But I haven't received the full benefit.

ALVI. Receive the full benefit some other time. Now, start counting.

SAM. Okay. (*HE finishes chanting.*) I'll count. (*HE stands up.*)

ALVI. And keep counting. Don't let your mind wander the way it usually does.

SAM. My mind doesn't wander.

ALVI. It wanders all the time.

SAM. Occasionally it drifts. But it doesn't wander.

ALVI. Whatever it does, don't do it today. You ready to start?

SAM. Yeah. I'm ready.

ALVI. Good. Lets go. (*Shouts.*) Rawlings, XP61.

SAM. Seven.

ALVI. Wilson, A2000.

SAM. Four.

ALVI. Spalding, XP70.

SAM. Eight.

ALVI. Spalding, XP6000.

SAM. Twenty.

ALVI. (*Stops. Amazed.*) How can we still have twenty XP6000's?

SAM. We didn't sell any.

ALVI. I told you to push them.

SAM. I pushed. Nobody bought.

ALVI. (*Pause. Change in tone.*) I don't understand it, Sammy. I order two George Brett's, they're gone in an hour. I buy twenty XP6000's, nobody touches them for months.

SAM. People buy different things these days. You have to check your customers all the time. Otherwise, you'll be selling the wrong things to the wrong people and losing money.

ALVI. You saying I don't know what I'm ordering?

SAM. I said we have to watch what's moving. No need to get steamed.

ALVI. (*Steamed.*) Who's getting steamed?

SAM. Every time we take stock, it's the same thing. You get steamed. I get steamed. And, before you know it, we're fighting. (*Pause. SAM looks around. Frightened.*) What was that noise?

ALVI. What noise?

SAM. From the storeroom.

ALVI. What did it sound like?

SAM. A thump.

ALVI. Hear it any more?

SAM. No.

ALVI. Maybe it went away.

SAM. A thump doesn't just go away. I've got good ears.

ALVI. If you're so sure you heard it, go into the storeroom and check it out.

SAM. I'm not going in there.

ALVI. What's wrong? You scared?

SAM. No. I just don't like poking around in dark places.

ALVI. Why not?

SAM. Cause I don't know what I'll find.

ALVI. Take a bat.

SAM. A what?

ALVI. A Louisville Slugger. Flip on the lights, and when the thumper comes out, bop him one on the head.

SAM. If you're so smart, you go down and do it.

ALVI. I didn't hear a thump.

SAM. It doesn't matter. You brought it up. You do the bopping. It's a rule of the game.

ALVI. What game's that?

SAM. It's called bop the thumper. I just made it up.

ALVI. There you go. Making things up. Letting your mind wander. If I wandered like you wander, we'd have wandered out of here years ago because we'd never sell anything.

SAM. Come on, Alvi. I talk to people. Make then happy. And along the way, I sell the goods. And at selling the goods, Sammy Baker's an artist supreme. You know why? Because I listen to people. You'd be surprised how many people don't listen to anyone but themselves. They look like they're listening, but they're thinking about something else. Or drifting off someplace. And that's where they make their mistake. Because if you don't listen to what a person has to say, you don't know what they want. And if you don't know what they want, you can't give them what they need. And if you can't give them what they need, you don't sell the goods. Know what I mean?

ALVI. (*Not listening.*) What?

SAM. I said, know what I mean?

ALVI. You know something? Ever since you started taking those night school courses, you've been nothing but hot air and theories twenty-four hours a day. Psychology. Art. Fancy magazines. That's not what guys like us do.

SAM. Oh yeah? What do we do?

ALVI. Read the sports pages. Watch the Mets on the tube.

SAM. These courses are better than that. They add to your store of knowledge.

ALVI. Can they tell you what the new rent's going to be?

SAM. Not that kind of knowledge. They give you knowledge of ... yourself. (*Pause.*) When we were kids, I was no student. Wasn't a girl getter. Not even a ballplayer. They used to call me Slow Sammy, remember? The guy who'd get there huffing and puffing a little after everyone else. When Bernice was alive, she laughed at my jokes and made a fuss about how I looked like Robert Mitchum when we went out dancing. But I felt she was saying those things just to pump me up. Because, she knew, inside, I felt like a big nothing. (*Change.*) I'm thinking thoughts in these classes I never dreamed I'd think. I'm reading books, Alvi. Listening to symphonies. All of a sudden, I have ideas, opinions. (*Pause.*) You should come to class some Tuesday. I'm taking philosophy this term. Be good for you to use your noodle a little.

ALVI. I use my noodle all the time. What do you do in this class?

SAM. We discuss how to act ethical.

ALVI. Act ethical, you get your ass handed to you.

SAM. Not in business, Alvi. In life.

ALVI. Business. Life. Same thing. Only business is more predictable.

SAM. Here. I'll give you an example. You're walking down the street. It's a nice day like today, you're enjoying the sun, maybe eating an ice cream cone or munching on a danish, when, all of a sudden, a thousand dollar bill drops out of the pocket of the guy walking in front of you and flutters down to the sidewalk right at your feet. There's no one behind you. No one on the side. The whole block is silent and empty. And there's that lonely bill, lying green and peaceful in the summer sun. (*Pause.*) Now ...

ALVI. I swoop in like Pee Wee Reese on a grounder, pocket the dough, and walk down the street without so much as breaking my stride.

SAM. Okay. But you have to ask yourself, if everyone did what you did, what kind of a world would we live in?

ALVI. We live in a world of crooks. Besides, if a guy's dropping thousand dollar bills like they were lint from his pocket, he can afford to take a loss. (*Pause.*) You don't have to go to night school to know that. Just use your noodle. (*Back to ledger books.*) Now, how about taking stock.

SAM. Have some coffee first.

ALVI. Coffee makes me nervous.

SAM. Never used to make you nervous. First thing I'd do in the old days was put a nice fresh pot of coffee on the hotplate. You couldn't start the day without a cup.

ALVI. That was a long time ago. Now one cup and I'm up all night.

SAM. But you still like a danish.

ALVI. I'm not hungry.

SAM. Come on. (*Holds out two danish.*) I have cheese and prune.

ALVI. (*Considers. Hesitates. Gives in.*) Give me a prune. I'll nibble between shouts.

(SAM hands him a danish. THEY bite.)

ALVI. Chest protectors.

SAM. Six. (*Goes behind counter to items.*)

ALVI. Catcher's masks.

SAM. Seven small.

ALVI. Medium?

SAM. Eight.

ALVI. (*Stops. Looks at danish.*) Where'd you get this danish?

SAM. The French place up the street.

ALVI. It stinks.

SAM. (*Takes another bite.*) Tastes okay to me.

ALVI. Everything tastes okay to you. But I know danish. (*Pause.*) You know why we're in trouble, Sammy? This neighborhood's messing up our sales. (*Pause.*) How many Clinchers?

SAM. (*Searches.*) Fifteen.

ALVI. Batting tees.

SAM. A case of Dwight Gooden's just came in. (*Pause.*) The neighborhood's fine. New stores. Interesting people.

ALVI. It's not fine. It's rotten. Lousy. (*Pause.*) Shin guards?

SAM. (*Counts.*) Eight.

ALVI. The old feeling's gone, Sammy. The new people who come in here. They don't

appreciate service, they don't care about the
personal touch. They don't even understand
sports. I had a guy in here the other morning.
Couldn't have been more than twenty-five. This
kid, this baby, signs for three hundred dollars on
a Gold Card to sweat his ass off running in the
park. Eighty-dollar shoes. Five-dollar socks.
Thirty-dollar shirts. As though all that crap's
going to make him run any faster. (*Pause.*) These
new people may have money in their pockets, but
they don't know the first thing about sports.
Sports isn't fancy shoes and shirts. Sports is
people. And sweating and cheering and patting
asses and locker room bullshit and arguing
averages till your throat turns sore. That's what
sports is. And if you don't know that, you know
nothing. This neighborhood stinks, if you ask
me. (*Takes a bite of danish.*) And so does this
goddamned danish.

(*Pause. SAM begins arranging football helmets
    nearby.*)

ALVI. Basketballs.

(*No answer. SAM admires the helmets.*)

ALVI. (*Louder.*) Basketballs.
SAM. The helmets look nice here, don't they?
ALVI. There you go. Wandering again.
SAM. I wasn't wandering. I was …

ALVI. You were wandering onto helmets when I wanted basketballs. Helmets are helmets. They look the same no matter where they are.

SAM. Not true, Alvi. Helmets are important. *Small Business News.* April issue. They said you should always put brightly colored objects, like helmets, near the door because bright colors lead the eye inside.

ALVI. I don't care about your magazines and I don't care about helmets. Understand? I only care about basketballs. How many we got?

SAM. (*HE counts a long time.*) Thirty-three.

ALVI. (*Amazed.*) Thirty-three?

SAM. The Community Center. They cancelled the order. You were supposed to call Spalding and send them back.

ALVI. I was?

SAM. A couple of months ago.

ALVI. I don't remember.

SAM. Then you forgot.

ALVI. You think they'll take them back after all this time?

SAM. I'm not sure.

ALVI. What'll we do with thirty-three basketballs?

SAM. Call Manny at Camp Rapapo. He's stocking up for the summer.

ALVI. Yeah, Sammy. Good thinking. Manny'll take them off our hands. (*Pause.*) I hope.

SAM. (*Hands ALVI another danish.*) Try the other danish. Maybe cheese is better.

ALVI. (*Examines it.*) It's no better. I can tell from looking. (*Pause.*) See Angela last night, Sammy?

SAM. Maybe I did. Maybe I didn't.

ALVI. That means you did. Was it good?

SAM. You mean dinner?

ALVI. I don't mean dinner. I mean after dinner. At home. With the lights down low and Sinatra spinning soft on the turntable.

SAM. You know I'm not going to talk, so why ask me every day?

ALVI. I'm curious. That's all. Old guy like you and a pretty young woman like Angela. Just wanted to know what it was like. I haven't been with a young woman since I was a young man. And then, I was too young to appreciate what being with a young woman's like. So I'd like to share your experience.

SAM. My experience is my business.

ALVI. How about a story, like we used to tell.

SAM. We told stories forty years ago. And half of them were bullshit.

ALVI. Every story I told was true.

SAM. Come on.

ALVI. Every single one. There was a time, Sammy. (*Pause.*) There was a time … (*Pause.*) We got hardballs?

SAM. Yeah, we got hardballs.

ALVI. How many?

SAM. Twelve on the floor and two cases in the storeroom.

ALVI. How about it, Sammy?

SAM. How about what?

ALVI. A story to start the day.

SAM. You want stories? Buy *Penthouse Forum*.

ALVI. Come on, Sammy. If two guys can't talk about women, what the hell can they talk about?

SAM. It's a big world, Alvi. There's a million things to talk about.

ALVI. But nothing quite as interesting as you and Angela in the sack.

SAM. Drop it, Alvi.

ALVI. Drop what?

SAM. (*Angry.*) Just drop it, okay?

ALVI. Okay. It's dropped. (*Pause.*) Spaldings. Where are they?

SAM. You didn't order them.

ALVI. Of course I ordered them.

SAM. You were about to order them, then a lady came in for running shoes, and you never did.

ALVI. Why didn't you remind me?

SAM. I tried. You said you ordered them, then you stormed off to the storeroom.

ALVI. I'm checking in back.

SAM. I'm telling you. We don't ...

ALVI. Don't tell me. I'll see for myself.

SAM. Be my guest.

(*ALVI goes to storeroom. SAM starts to count. Loses interest and begins dancing the mambo in front of mirror.*)

ALVI. (*From storeroom.*) What are you doing out there, Sammy?

SAM. Practicing. The singles club dance is tonight. Remember? I'm in the mambo contest. With Angela.

ALVI. (*From storeroom.*) You'll win. No problem. You were born to mambo. So stop dancing and start counting. Howie'll be here any minute.

SAM. (*Pause. Lost in memory.*) A red organdy dress. With matching shoes and bag. When she wore her dancing organdy, hair loose and smelling green as summer, I thought we'd dance forever.

ALVI. (*Returns.*) Nothing, Sammy. We've got nothing.

SAM. (*Still lost.*) What?

ALVI. Not a single Spalding left. Christ, Sammy. I can't do anything right these days.

(*Pause.*)

SAM. (*Still lost in his revery.*) Do you ever think about Bernice, Alvi?

ALVI. (*Thoughtful.*) Sure I do, Sammy. I thought about her just now, in fact. Seeing you dancing. I remember when you and Bernice danced together in the old days, people would stop cold on the floor to watch. Just like Fred and Ginger in the movies.

SAM. I miss her, Alvi. Seven years and Angela and all the changes and I miss her bad as ever. Some days, I even expect her to walk in here the way she used to in the old days. With a tuna salad sandwich for my lunch or a sweater I left at home. Or a joke she heard from Gilbert at the candy store.

ALVI. She'd tell a joke, and laugh that little girl laugh, and you'd think she'd be young forever.

SAM. (*Pause.*) No one stays young forever. But some people have a chance to grow old. (*Pause.*) Come on. What's next?

ALVI. (*Concerned.*) You okay, Sammy?

SAM. Yeah. Yeah. I'm fine.

ALVI. You sure?

SAM. Sure, Alvi. I'm fine. Let's count Gary Carters. (*HE goes behind counter and begins to count.*) Four. Five. Six. We got seven.

ALVI. I've got nine here. When did we sell two?

SAM. We didn't.

ALVI. So where are they?

SAM. Saturday was my nephews' birthday. The twins. Eddie and Jimmy. You can't give one a present without giving the same thing to the other. So I took two Gary Carters. I left you a note on the register.

ALVI. I didn't see it.

SAM. Maybe you didn't look.

ALVI. I always look. (*Checks on register.*) If it was there, I would have seen it.

SAM. Are you saying I took them without telling you?

ALVI. No. I'm just wondering how much of our stock ends up in your nephews' house.

SAM. (*Hurt.*) I've never taken a thing from this store without telling you.

ALVI. (*Apologetic.*) You're right, Sammy. You wouldn't do a thing like that.

SAM. Then why'd you say it?

ALVI. (*Pause.*) I don't know. I'm confused. My nerves are on edge. For forty years I've made this store work. I'd make an adjustment here, tighten a little there, and everything was fine. But these days, things are changing too fast. (*Pause.*) We'll never do enough volume to pay the kind of rent Howie could ask. And if we can't pay the rent, we lose the store. And if we lose the store, I don't know what I'll do.

SAM. We've got enough to retire.

ALVI. You want to retire?

SAM. No.

ALVI. So why mention it?

SAM. You used to talk retirement all the time.

ALVI. When was that?

SAM. I don't know when. All the time. Jai-lai and deep-sea fishing and horses at the track and saying good-bye to the dirt and the noise.

ALVI. When was the last time I talked retirement?

SAM. Come to think it, not for a while.

ALVI. Damn right, Sammy. I changed my mind about retirement last April after Harriet and I went to Florida for seven fun-filled days and nights under tropical skies. (*Pause.*) Something happened to me down there, Sammy. I didn't tell anyone.

SAM. What do you mean?

ALVI. I had ... a revelation. One Monday morning on the mezzanine level of the Sea Breeze Mall in Hallendale. Harriet was looking for summer tops and coordinates at the Sand and Surf Boutique across from the artificial waterfall with the tropical fish pond underneath. I sat waiting on a flaming orange plastic bench with piped-in John Denver songs playing in my ears. And you know what I saw? Men, Sammy. An endless procession of men my age shuffling three feet behind their wives, lugging shopping bags and boxes. (*Pause.*) Everywhere I looked, there were men. Thousands of men. Coming from every direction. Like zombies, Sammy. Staring. Shuffling. Not saying a word. And when I looked closely, every one of those old men looked exactly like me. (*Pause.*) Then it happened.

SAM. What?

ALVI. All of a sudden, I was standing on the edge of the tropical fish pond, waving my arms wild and screaming "I will not die in a mall. I WILL NOT DIE IN A MALL." (*Pause.*) When they spotted me screaming it was Red Alert in Paradise. Security guards from every direction. Hats flying off their heads, walkie-talkies crackling. They thought they had a psycho on their hands. And, believe me, the one thing they hate more than litter at the Sea Breeze Mall are psychos. Before I know it, two big security guys grab me from behind and start applying a half-nelson. At that moment, Harriet comes walking out of the Sand and Surf Boutique, two shopping bags filled with pastel tops and matching skirts. She sees the security guys and she runs over shouting and punching. They figure they have two psychos on their hands. A husband and wife psycho team. But they aren't going to rough up a woman. Not with a dozen old men gawking at them in their Bermuda shorts. So five guards, revolvers by their sides, escort us real polite to the main entrance, the one with the palm trees growing through the floor, and throw us out. I'm standing in front of the Sea Breeze Mall and I vow, right then, that no matter how old I got, or how sick or how lonely, I'd never be one of those old men rotting like avocadoes in the Florida sun.

SAM. (*Pause.*) So that's what happened to retirement, huh?

ALVI. That's what happened to retirement. Gone in a mall.

SAM. Glad to hear it.

ALVI. Yeah? How come?

SAM. It hurt me to think you could walk away from the store so easy. One, two, three and you're dealing pinochle under the palm trees.

ALVI. (*With feeling.*) I can't walk away, Sammy. I need this store. It's going to kill me to hear Howie say he's raising us five hundred percent. It's going to kill me dead.

SAM. When Howie comes, let me do the talking. Understand?

ALVI. You expect me to stand around smiling while he rips this store out of our hands?

SAM. I'm the salesman. Leave the talking to me.

ALVI. You talk too much.

SAM. Says who?

ALVI. Says me. I've seen you. A hundred times. A customer makes up his mind to buy, you start bending his ear about the Mets or the weather, and the next thing you know, he changes his mind and he's gone. (*Pause.*) There's a time and a place for talking, Sammy. Remember that when Howie comes.

SAM. Don't worry, Alvi. I know what I'm doing

ALVI. What you're doing is driving me crazy.

SAM. You need to create a pleasant atmosphere before you do business. It was in the tips section of *Business Week* just last month.

ALVI. Maybe we should call Ernie the Florist for some cut flowers to put around the place. Christ, Sammy. You'll believe anything as long as it's printed in one of those magazines. (*Checks watch.*) It's nearly ten. We've got hours more inventory. Let's take stock while we still have stock to take. Jerseys first. Then jackets and hats. (*Pause.*) Redskins.

(*No answer from SAM who's thinking.*)

ALVI. I said REDSKINS!

SAM. Did my mambo look okay before?

ALVI. What kind of question is that? We're counting Redskins.

SAM. No matter how much I practice, it never feels right.

ALVI. It looked fine, Sammy. All you need is a little confidence. Let's get back to counting.

SAM. You think so?

ALVI. Yeah. I think so. How many Redskins?

SAM. I can't count when I'm thinking about my mambo.

ALVI. Okay, Sammy. Listen. I'm taking five minutes to deal with the mambo crisis. Then we count and you don't wander. Get it?

SAM. Yeah. I get it.

ALVI. Good. I know what you're doing wrong.

SAM. You do?

ALVI. You're thinking too much. (*HE holds out his arms in dance position.*) Come over here. Hold me like you hold Angela. And I'll show you.

SAM. I can't do that.

ALVI. Why not?

SAM. Someone might see.

ALVI. So someone'll see. Who cares?

SAM. What do I do?

ALVI. Come over here. Like I told you.

(*SAM comes over to Alvi and assumes a dancing position.*)

SAM. Okay. I'm here.

ALVI. Now. The secret of dancing is to feel the rhythm and let your feet follow. Automatic. Close your eyes and imagine what I tell you now.

SAM. Come on …

ALVI. Trust me, Sammy. I know what I'm doing. Close your eyes. (*SAM closes his eyes.*) Good. Very good. Now imagine this. It's a summer night. 1955. You're twenty-five years old and deep in love. You got on your best sharkskin suit and a brand new pair of Florsheims. You got Bernice in your arms. You walk onto the floor. The music starts. One … two … three. And. One … two … three. And.

(*THEY begin dancing. SAM's eyes are closed. HE dances freely, imagining.*)

ALVI. That's it, Sammy. You're getting it.

(*ALVI sings a mambo tune as THEY glide around the store. THEY continue dancing, inspired. As THEY dance, a man in his early thirties appears at the door. HE wears an elaborate running suit and the fanciest pair of sneakers you ever saw. HE wears a shiny gold necklace. HE watches the mamboers and makes a SOUND to get their attention. THEY dance on, blissfully unaware of HIM.*)

HOWIE. Hello.

(THEY continue dancing.)

HOWIE. I said hello!

SAM. (*Snaps out of trance.*) Hey, Howie. I didn't hear you come in. How you doing?

HOWIE. I'm doing okay. How are Arthur and Katherine Murray?

SAM. Fine, Howie. Fine.

HOWIE. I'm not interrupting anything, am I?

SAM. No. Alvi was just helping me out with the mambo.

HOWIE. You start off every day with a mambo?

SAM. That's Howie for you. Always joking. I'm in a mambo contest tonight. Alvi's giving me some pointers.

ALVI. That's right. I'm his personal trainer.

SAM. (*To Howie.*) That's some jogging suit you're wearing.

HOWIE. Two hundred bucks at Runner's World.

SAM You hear that, Alvi? We should order some.

HOWIE. You sure? This is top of the line.

ALVI. What's wrong? We can't handle top of the line?

HOWIE. Did I say that?

SAM. (*Intervening.*) Howie means we carry more moderately priced items. Don't you, Howie?

HOWIE. Yeah. That's all I mean. (*Notices baseball gloves on display.*) Hey, look at these gloves. New models come in?

SAM. Oh, yeah, Howie. Bunch of autographs. Go ahead. Check them out.

(HOWIE looks as SAM speaks)

SAM. You know, Howie. I might order a couple of those jogging suits for the store. I always say, a man in business has to keep up with the times. Just the other day I was reading *New York* magazine. A whole issue on "Executive Lifestyles and the Men Who Lead Them." You read that issue Alvi?

ALVI. I'm afraid I missed it.

SAM. It was something. (*To Alvi.*) What do you think they get for a cup of coffee at one of those power breakfasts downtown?

ALVI. How should I know?

SAM. Howie knows. He's been there.

HOWIE. (*Checking out gloves.*) Been where?

SAM. At those power breakfasts downtown. When you made that big deal with the developer from the Island, you signed the papers at a power breakfast at the Regency Hotel. Right?

HOWIE. How do you know that?

SAM. You told me all about it.

HOWIE. You should have been there, Sam. It was beautiful. A work of art. First I told a couple of jokes, just to loosen him up. Break the ice. He ordered a mimosa. I ordered tomato juice.

Straight. He had Eggs Benedict. I had the
Florentine. Then he made his mistake. He ordered
a second mimosa and I knew he was mine. I
waited for a moment of weakness. And I nailed
him. I owe it all to you.

SAM. To me?

HOWIE. Yeah. To you. When I was a kid, I'd
sit in this store all day Saturday listening to you
talk and sell and tell jokes. It was like listening to
an artist.

SAM. You hear that, Alvi? He listened to me
talk. And he liked it. Did I wander too much,
Howie?

HOWIE. Are you kidding? You were beautiful.
Stories. Jokes. Statistics. And all the time, selling
the goods. I remember saying to myself, if I could
talk half as sweet as Sammy Baker when I grow
up, I could sell anything to anyone. (*Pause*.)
Know what I'm selling today? Health clubs all
over Jersey. Iron City Health and Fitness Centers.
The name have a ring?

SAM. I like it. Yeah. It definitely has a ring.
Coffee?

HOWIE. I had at home. New cappuccino
machine. Imported.

SAM. A danish? Fresh this morning?

HOWIE. I hate danish.

ALVI. Danish isn't good enough anymore.
Right, Howie?

HOWIE. Come on Alvi, don't have an attitude.
I haven't talked to you guys since my father

retired. I'm glad we have an opportunity. If you have questions or problems, I'm the man to see.

SAM. I'm glad you're the man. Because I respect you, Howie. Not only as a businessman, but as a person. And I know you respect Alvi and me. I always say, no matter how successful a guy gets, if he forgets his past, he's in trouble. Don't I always say that, Alvi?

ALVI. Yeah, Sam. You say that every day.

HOWIE. I'm not going to have the time to talk the way my father did. I have meetings, appointments ...

SAM. It's okay, Howie. When I was your age, I didn't want to talk to old guys either. One day, you'll be the guy the young guys don't want to talk to. It's a big circle.

HOWIE. Don't get me wrong, Sam. I love talking to you guys. Sometimes I wish I could just hang around here all day talking the way I did when I was a kid.

SAM. Why don't you come in some time late in the day? We could have chinese sent in and watch a Mets game.

HOWIE. I can't, Sam.

SAM. Why not?

HOWIE. I'm not a kid anymore. (*Pause.*) Listen to this. You won't believe it. Jennifer got into the Trent School.

SAM. No kidding? That's a hard school to get into.

HOWIE. I knew she would. She's a gifted child. (*Proud.*) She scored in the top one percent of all four-year-olds in the country. Verbal and mathematical. And she has exceptional small motor skills. Plus musical talent. We started her on violin. Three days a week with some Japanese lady on the East Side. (*HE takes out photo. Shows it to them.*) When I see her in her little white dress carrying her violin case, I can't stop myself from crying.

SAM. I always knew Jennifer was gifted.

HOWIE. You did?

SAM. Sure. Some kids have light in their eyes, some kids don't. Jennifer has light in her eyes. Just like you when you were a kid.

HOWIE. (*Panicked.*) Jesus Christ. (*HE rushes out.*)

SAM. Where's he going like that?

ALVI. Who cares. Snotnose little bastard. (*Pause.*) Stop making small talk, Sammy. I'm going crazy waiting to hear the new rent.

SAM. I'm softening him up. Creating the atmosphere. Didn't you hear him say he loves to hear me talk?

ALVI. He hasn't been your partner for forty years. Create the atmosphere a little quicker.

HOWIE. (*Returns. Out of breath.*) Safe. It's safe.

SAM. You get a ticket or something?

HOWIE. No. Just checking my car phone. They smash the window and rip them out right under your nose. I already lost two this year.

SAM. You have a car phone?

HOWIE. State of the art. Twelve hundred bucks.

SAM. What for?

HOWIE. What do you mean, what for? You have to have one.

SAM. Why?

HOWIE. I don't know. Everyone has one. If I don't have one, I fall behind.

SAM. Behind who?

HOWIE. They guys who have them.

SAM. Who are they?

HOWIE. The competition. Fall behind the competition and you never catch up. I hardly use it, but it makes me feel good knowing it's there. Know what I mean?

SAM. No. I don't. A car's one of the few places a guy can be alone with his thoughts. I wouldn't interrupt that with a phone.

HOWIE. (*Checks his watch.*) It's getting late. And I have good news. (*Picks up briefcase. Crosses to counter.*)

ALVI. You do?

HOWIE. Yeah. You've got a new lease. (*Opens briefcase. Takes out lease.*)

ALVI. That's good news?

HOWIE. I didn't have to offer you one. Landlords are denying leases all over town. But I couldn't do that to you guys. And you'll be happy to know I'm only raising you three hundred percent.

SAM. Three hundred percent?

HOWIE. You have to give old friends a break.

ALVI. That's a little steep. Don't you think?

HOWIE. Believe me. That's a bargain basement number. The median rent in this neighborhood's seven thousand a month. With the increase, you'll only be paying forty-eight hundred. Adjust that for inflation over the ten-year life of the lease, and you're way ahead of the game.

SAM. Things have been a little slow, Howie. Seasonal adjustment. Spring slump.

HOWIE. They'll pick up.

SAM. I don't think they will this time. A hundred-fifty we might be able to handle, but this...

HOWIE. Come on, Sam. I'm being fair, you have to be fair. I'm losing money at three hundred percent. I can't go any lower than that. For anyone else, it would have been five hundred percent. (*Looks at his watch. Closes briefcase.*) I have to get going. I have a meeting in Jersey at eleven.

SAM. Listen, Howie ...

HOWIE. I can't talk now. I have to go. I'm not trying to screw you. Three hundred percent's a good offer. Think about it. Work out the numbers. I'll come back next week for the lease. You got questions, call my office. One of the secretaries can help you out. (*Shakes Alvi's hand.*)

ALVI. Thanks a lot, Howie.

HOWIE. (*HE turns to leave. Looks again at the gloves.*) Listen, Sam. Do you mind if I take one of these mitts home for Zachy? He's starting Little League next week. I want him to do good.

SAM. Sure, Howie. Whatever you want.

HOWIE. (*Takes one.*) Thanks, Sam. You're a pal. (*Shakes his hand.*) I'll tell you all about the game when I come for the lease. Got to go. The tunnel's a bitch this time of day. (*Bangs glove.*) Nice pocket. Real nice pocket. (*HOWIE leaves.*)

ALVI. (*Long pause.*) That's it, Sammy. We're through. (*Pause.*) Why'd you give him that glove?

SAM. What do you mean, why?

ALVI. I mean, he walks in here, raises us three hundred percent and you give him a brand new glove as a bonus?

SAM. So I gave him a glove. Big deal.

ALVI. It is a big deal. You're always doing things like that.

SAM. Like what?

ALVI. Giving things away for no reason. If I didn't watch you, you'd give away the whole goddamned store.

SAM. Come on, Alvi. That's not true. A little generosity builds good will. Improves customer relations. I was just reading in ...

ALVI. I don't want to hear what you've been reading. Good will's going to do nothing for us now. We're beyond good will. Three hundred percent is forty-eight hundred a month. We're paying twelve hundred and barely managing now. A year from now there'll be an ice cream store here. Or a cookie stand. Or some designer jean emporium. (*Pause*.) It's all over, Sammy. All over.

SAM. No it's not.

ALVI. Tell me how we're going to manage forty-eight hundred a month?

SAM. I've got a couple of ideas in my head ...

ALVI. Don't give me that night-school bullshit.

SAM. This is no bullshit. It's scientific. We can make it if we renovate.

ALVI. What are you talking about? Renovate.

SAM. I've been doing research. I talked to Eddie down at Clothes and Things. Last year he renovated. This year, he tripled his volume. He says we could do the same thing here.

ALVI. We're not selling skirts and tops. We're selling sporting goods.

SAM. The same principles apply. The more merchandise you display on the floor, the more volume you do, the more profit you take home. According to *Modern Business Methods* it's called the Bloomingdale's Formula (*Pause*.) Understand what I'm saying?

ALVI. Let's say I'm listening. (*HE sits*.)

SAM. We've go two thousand square feet of raw footage. And we only use seven hundred for display. It we renovate we can increase it to fifteen hundred. According to the Bloomingdale's Formula, we'll be increasing our profits by over a hundred percent. And if we advertise in the right places, we could do even better. I have all the numbers. Sit down with your calculator and you'll see it can work.

ALVI. I don't like changing things, Sammy. (*Pause.*) I like dust. And clutter. I like to run my hand over the counter and feel dirt beneath my fingers. My dirt. Our dirt. The dirt of forty years. (*Pause.*) You figure what a job like that'll cost?

SAM. Twenty thousand. Fixtures and lighting included. Eddie told me.

ALVI. (*Pause.*) Where do we get that kind of money?

SAM. Our IRA's just matured. We each take out ten thousand.

ALVI. That's retirement money.

SAM. But you don't want to retire.

ALVI. So what? You don't touch retirement money.

SAM. Says who?

ALVI. It's one of the three commandments of life. Don't go into your principal. Don't borrow what you can't pay back. Don't touch retirement money.

SAM. Think of it as an investment in the future. (*Pause.*) We'll apply modern methods, Alvi. Advertising. Marketing. The works. I can see the ads already. Come to the all new Sam and Alvi's. The modern store with the old-fashioned touch. The place'll be beautiful. We could do volume we never imagined. We could have people in here from Jersey. From the island. From Connecticut even.

ALVI. I don't want people in here from those places. I hate people from those places. I want things to stay the way they are.

SAM. They can't stay that way. Times change. Stores have to change too.

ALVI. I don't want to change. Can't you understand that?

SAM. And you don't want to retire either.

ALVI. That's right, Sammy. To retire is to die.

SAM. Then what do you want to do?

ALVI. I don't know.

SAM. You have to know.

ALVI. I don't know, Sammy. I just don't know.

BLACKOUT

End of Act I

ACT II

*One week later. A few things have been
rearranged. The place looks a little brighter.
LIGHTS rise on SAM sipping a cup of coffee
at the counter and reading a magazine. ALVI
enters, looking for a lost object. HE mutters to
himself as HE picks up invoices, drops them
down, lifts merchandise, doesn't find what
he's looking for, continues searching. SAM
watches Alvi.*

SAM. What are you looking for?

ALVI. My pen.

SAM. Which one?

ALVI. I only have one. Blue top. Silver
bottom. Push it and it clicks. You see it? (*Lifts up
more papers.*)

SAM. It's not on your desk?

ALVI. If it was there, would I be looking for
it?

SAM. Pants pockets?

ALVI. No.

SAM. Jacket?

ALVI. Who wears a jacket on a day like this?
It's eighty degrees out there.

SAM. (*Hands HIM a pen.*) No big deal. Use
mine.

ALVI. I can't.

SAM. Why not?

ALVI. That's my lucky pen. If I work with another pen, the numbers don't come out right.

SAM. You know what they say about people who can only do things one way?

ALVI. I don't care what they say, I want my pen.

SAM. They say they're incapable of dealing with the present so they seek security in familiar objects from the past. There was an article just last month in *Science Digest*. Explained the whole thing.

ALVI. How many times have I told you, I don't want to hear about magazines. (*Searches.*) Where he hell's my pen?

SAM. When I finish this article, I'll look for your pen.

ALVI. You can finish the article anytime. I need my pen now.

SAM. Check your desk?

ALVI. Of course I checked my desk. That's what bothers me. Every night, before I leave, I put my pen on top of my ledger book. Tip facing the door. This morning, I look, and it's nowhere to be found.

SAM. (*Notices something.*) Hey, Alvi. What's that in your shirt?

ALVI. Where?

SAM. Front pocket.

ALVI. (*Looks down sees pen in his pocket.*) My pen. Thanks. (*Pause.*) Back to the numbers.

(*Sits down on stool, works with adding machine.*)

SAM. The numbers are the same no matter how many times you count them.

ALVI. Humor me then. And let me count. Once we sign that lease, there's no turning back. You understand that, don't you?

SAM. Sure I do. But you applied the Bloomingdale's Formula.

ALVI. What is that, magic? One, two, three and everything's fine?

SAM. I'm not saying it's magic. All I'm saying is we can handle three hundred percent.

ALVI. Forget it, Sammy. (*Pause.*) Sometimes, I wish he'd raised us four hundred percent like he raised Millie. At least then, we'd know we were through. This way, it's a slow death figuring angles.

SAM. I'm telling you, we'll do okay if we renovate.

ALVI. How do you know? You read it in your horoscope in *Cosmo*?

SAM. No. Last night I had a dream. You and me are standing in the store on a beautiful summer day. But instead of wearing pants and shirts, we're wearing pedal pushers and old-fashioned wigs. Then a guy walks in looking exactly like Howie Golden. This guy's carrying a piece of parchment. He spreads the parchment on the counter, and we sign our names, with old-fashioned, feather quill pens. When the guy signs, I look over his shoulder and there, in an enormous scrawl, is the name ... John Hancock.

ALVI. Yeah? And then?

SAM. Then I woke up.

ALVI. A dream like that tells you to renovate?

SAM. If you understand its significance.

ALVI. I understand its significance. Did we pay the insurance this month? (*Takes out check register.*)

SAM. You wrote the check yourself. Why you asking?

ALVI. Here's the significance. The parchment's our policy. And John Hancock's the insurance man come to cancel on us because we can't afford the premiums.

SAM. He's not the insurance man.

ALVI. Then who is he?

SAM. I don't know exactly. But when I woke up this morning, I felt light-headed. Like I could run twice around the reservoir without getting winded.

ALVI. Come on. I feel light-headed every time I pay the bills. Happy to be free of debt for another month. People believe what they want to believe and make up dreams to convince themselves they're right.

SAM. No way, Alvi. A dream's as real as anything in this world. That dream told me we made the right decision. It was like seeing into the future.

ALVI. I don't want to see into the future. When I think about the future, I see myself laid out in a box, (*HE slams check register shut.*) or shuffling behind a walker. These days, I'm thinking more and more about the past. It comes on when I'm doing my numbers. I'm sitting here, thinking and figuring, and all of a sudden, I'm somewhere else, somewhere I haven't been for years. (*Pause.*) Remember the fifty-three series, Sammy?

SAM. Sure. We drove together to the seventh game. All the way down Bedford Avenue in your old Dodge convertible.

ALVI. Everything was perfect that day, wasn't it? The sun high above the stands. The sound of the crowd around us. I felt young, Sammy. So young I thought I'd never grow old. When I breathed that bleacher air I was breathing sun and light and hot dog steam and everything I ever loved. (*Pause.*) I made a wish that day. I wished that the game would never end. That it would go into extra innings and the innings would stretch into days and months and years and, through it all, we'd be sitting there, a pair of kids, out in the bleachers, rooting till the end of time. (*Pause.*) I know it makes sense to renovate. But I'm afraid that after people come in and rip this place apart, my past, my memories are going to disappear and everything I ever knew or loved will go with them.

SAM. I know just how you feel.

ALVI. No, you don't. (*Returns to adding machine.*)

SAM. Yes, I do. It scares me to change things too.

ALVI. Come on, Sammy. Your life fell apart when Bernice died. And what did you do? Built yourself another one. If Harriet died, I couldn't do that.

SAM. You think it was so easy?

ALVI. I don't know. I never done it.

SAM. You know, I spent the first year after Bernice died sitting like an old pillow on my couch flipping the cable and feeling sorry for myself. If it wasn't for my magazines, I'd still be sitting there.

ALVI. What do magazines have to do with it?

SAM. Everything, Alvi. Everything. Right after Bernice died, I subscribed to *Sports Illustrated* and *Ring* just to pass the time. They came on Tuesday. I read them in a hour and I needed more. So I subscribed to *Car and Driver* and *Field and Stream*. They came on Wednesday. Then I needed something for Thursday, so I ordered *Time* and *Newsweek*. Before I knew it, I was subscribing to forty or fifty magazines. They were coming three and four a day, Alvi. Magazines I never heard of before. *The Nation, The New Republic, Opera News*. I read them all, Alvi. Cover to cover. The more I read, the more I wanted to know. So I started taking courses. Chinese cooking. American Literature. Modern Art. It was at a lecture on "Art after the Bomb" at the New School that I met Angela.

ALVI. And look at you now. A man of style and learning cutting the mustard every night with a pretty young woman.

SAM. Yeah. Right.

ALVI. You are cutting the mustard, aren't you?

SAM. I told you. I don't want to talk about those things.

ALVI. Why not?

SAM. I just don't, okay? Here I am trying to make you feel better, and all you can think about is whether or not I'm cutting the mustard with Angela.

ALVI. Well? Are you?

SAM. Didn't you listen to a word I said?

ALVI. Sure. I did. Especially the words about Angela.

SAM. You really want to know? I'll tell you. Sometimes the mustard gets cut, sometimes it doesn't. Sometimes I can't even open the jar. Now you happy?

ALVI. You mean you're not cutting the mustard? And you led me to believe you were?

SAM. I didn't lead you to believe anything. You believe what you want to believe no matter what anyone tells you. That's the way you are. (*Pause.*) I don't want to talk about this anymore. I brought croissants and iced cappuccinos from the cafe. Want some? (*Goes to end of counter where there's a croissant and a cup.*)

ALVI. I don't eat croissants.

SAM. Why not?

ALVI. I don't like them.

SAM. You ever taste them?

ALVI. No.

SAM. How you know you don't like them?

ALVI. Some things you don't like without tasting them. Like croissants and white wine spritzers.

SAM. Try one. (*Hands HIM croissant.*)

ALVI. I said no. (*Pushes it away.*)

SAM. Come on. (*Hands it back.*)

ALVI. Stop pushing, Sammy. (*Pushes it away again.*)

SAM. Who's pushing?

ALVI. You are.

SAM. I never push.

ALVI. You've been pushing night school on me for years.

SAM. That's not pushing. That's sharing enthusiasm.

ALVI. I don't want to share your enthusiasm. You and your enthusiasm are pushing me into this renovation.

SAM. I'm not pushing.

ALVI. It wasn't my idea.

SAM. You have no ideas.

ALVI. I have plenty of ideas.

SAM. Like what?

ALVI. I don't know. Plenty.

SAM. You said you wanted to stay.

ALVI. What else could I have said?

SAM. You could have said you didn't.

ALVI. And then?

SAM. We would have done something else.

ALVI. Like what? I don't want to retire.

SAM. Found another place. Started over.

ALVI. Maybe I should have said no.

SAM. You still can.

ALVI. Oh yeah?

SAM. Yeah. (*Pause.*)

ALVI. Look, Sammy. I don't want to argue with you. Just be quiet and don't make noise. I have to concentrate.

SAM. I'll drink my cappuccino, eat my croissant, and you won't even know I'm here.

ALVI. Good.

(*SAM moves down counter. Takes out pad. Starts figuring and eating his croissant. ALVI figures.*)

ALVI. Cut it out.

SAM. What did I do now?

ALVI. You munched and then you mumbled.

SAM. I never mumble. And you can't munch a croissant.

ALVI. You mumbled just before. And you munched too. A couple of times. When you munch and mumble, I lose count.

SAM. Boy. Everything sets you off today.

ALVI. Look. I'm taking a big chance here. I'm not the kind of guy who takes chances.

SAM. You can say that again.

ALVI. What's that supposed to mean?

SAM. It means every time there's a little tension or a decision to be made, you get steamed.

ALVI. (*Steamed.*) Who's steamed?

SAM. You are. Look at you.

ALVI. I'm not steamed. I'm pissed.

SAM. There's a difference?

ALVI. Yeah. A big difference. You get steamed at something. Like a situation. But you get pissed at a person. Like you.

SAM. You're pissed at me?

ALVI. That's right. I am.

SAM. Why?

ALVI. I'm tired of hearing you talk and dream and munch and mumble.

SAM. As though I do nothing but talk all day.

ALVI. That's all you do. Talk and dream.

SAM. There's nothing wrong with dreaming, Alvi. I'd rather be dreaming than worrying over numbers all day.

ALVI. You would, huh?

SAM. Yeah, I would.

ALVI. If I don't worry, I don't sign. Then you can dream forever without me.

SAM. Fine. Silence you want. Silence you have. I'll just sit here quiet and look over my list.

ALVI. What list?

SAM. My list of special orders if we do the renovation.

ALVI. Since when do you make lists of special orders?

SAM. I just started.

ALVI. Let me see. (*Takes list.*) A thousand dollars? For what?

SAM. A sign.

ALVI. We have a sign.

SAM. We need a new one.

ALVI. Why?

SAM. Our sign doesn't do what a sign's supposed to do.

ALVI. A sign's supposed to hang on the wall.

SAM. Not according to *Modern Retailing*. *Modern Retailing,* September issue, says a sign creates an identity for a store. That's what the baseball mitt will do.

ALVI. The baseball mitt?

SAM. Imagine, Alvi. It's a Saturday morning early in summer. You're walking through the neighborhood thinking how you could use a new pair of sneakers or a sweatshirt or a whiffle ball and bat for the kids. Under normal circumstances, you wouldn't do anything about it. But then you turn the corner onto our block, and you see it— glowing in the distance.

ALVI. What? See what?

SAM. A giant fiberglass baseball mitt six-feet wide and eight-feet high hanging over our door. Across the center, in one-foot purple script letters, flash the words Sam and Alvi's Sports Shop, on and off, ten times a minute, twenty-four hours a day. You try to turn away, but you can't. The force of the sign pulls you in. And once you're in, you see other things you need—tennis racquets, baseballs, gloves. Soon, you can't help yourself. You're in the grip of what *Modern Retailing* calls the "The Consumer Trance." And before you know it …

ALVI. Okay, Sammy. I've heard enough.

SAM. What do you mean? It's a great idea. *Modern Retailing* says stores that change their image by changing their sign can look forward to up to five percent growth in sales. I'll get the issue if you like.

ALVI. I don't care about *Modern Retailing*. I'm not throwing away my retirement money on some baseball mitt sign.

SAM. A sign's important.

ALVI. What's important is paying the rent. (*Pause*.) Look, Sammy. If we're going to work together, we've got to get things straight. I'm the numbers man. You're the salesman. Just because you've taken a couple of night school courses doesn't mean you can take over my end of the business. When I say no sign, it's no sign.

SAM. I have ideas too.

ALVI. You can have all the ideas you want. But I have the last say.

SAM. That's not fair.

ALVI. That's how it is.

SAM. That's how it's been.

ALVI. And how it's going to stay.

SAM. Maybe I don't want it that way?

ALVI. You don't? Go someplace else.

(*Tense silence. THEY separate, ALVI to the counter and his adding machine, SAM to the connected chair. HOWIE enters with briefcase in lightweight, summer suit.*)

HOWIE. Hey, guys. Listen to this one. A man gets hit by a car. He's lying on the ground, a crowd around him, when an ambulance driver bends down and whispers, "Excuse me, sir. Are you comfortable?" The guy on the ground looks up, dazed, and says "I make a living." (*No response from SAM and ALVI.*) "I make a living." (*Still no response.*) Hey. Come on. That was funny.

SAM. Okay. It was funny.

ALVI. Yeah. A laugh riot.

HOWIE. What's wrong with you guys? Lose your sense of humor?

SAM. You caught us at a bad moment. (*Pause.*) How'd Zacky make out with the new glove? I bet he was perfect in the field.

HOWIE. He didn't do too good.

SAM. I thought he was starting at second?

HOWIE. He started. But he made four errors in the first two innings so they moved him to right. Zacky's not coordinated.

SAM. He's young. He needs practice.

HOWIE. I take him to the park every weekend. I tell him. Get down in front of the grounders. Follow the ball into your glove. But he's not coordinated.

SAM. Maybe baseball's not his game.

HOWIE. His sister's more coordinated than him. And she's four years old.

SAM. So what. He's sweet. He's intelligent.

HOWIE. Yeah. But he's not coordinated. (*Pause.*) You signed the lease, right? You checked it out. You saw it was fair?

SAM. It may be fair, but it's still high for us.

HOWIE. Do what everyone else is doing. Raise a glove here, hike up a sneaker there, and you'll do fine. But first you you have to sign the lease.

SAM. I got extra iced cappuccino. Want one?

HOWIE. How'd you know I like iced cappuccino?

ALVI. A man with sophisticated taste always appreciates iced cappuccino. Right, Alvi?

HOWIE. Every night I make myself one of these. On my machine. There's nothing like a nice iced cappuccino on a hot summer night. Makes you feel like you're in Europe. Sitting at one of those fancy sidewalk cafes watching the beautiful women walk by. (*Takes a sip.*) Superbamente, Sam. Sup-er-ba-ment-te! (*Pause.*) You guys aren't having second thoughts about a new lease are you?

ALVI. No. There's a few things we have to work out before we sign. Right, Sam?

SAM. You could put it that way.

ALVI. I just did.

HOWIE. You've had a week to work them out.

ALVI. (*Getting angry.*) Some things take longer than a week to decide. We're talking about forty years here.

HOWIE. No need to shout.

ALVI. Who's shouting?

SAM. Take it easy, Alvi. Howie's just asking a question.

ALVI. I know that.

HOWIE. I've got a franchise calling me every day dying to get into this space. I can't hold him off forever.

ALVI. You'd love to have us out of here, wouldn't you, Howie? You could raise the rent sky high.

HOWIE. As a matter of fact, I could subdivide and make three times what I'm making now. But I promised you a lease. And I keep my word. (*Pause.*) Listen. I don't mean to pry, but have you guys thought about retirement?

ALVI. Why you asking?

HOWIE. The way things are changing around the neighborhood, this might be the right time to pack it in, buy a condo someplace and enjoy yourselves.

SAM. It just so happens we discussed retirement the other day.

HOWIE. And?

ALVI. We're not interested.

HOWIE. You should see the condo my father's got in Boca. Two bedrooms. Terrace on the eighteenth green. Swimming pool. Tennis courts. Health club. The works.

ALVI. That's nice for your father, Howie. But we figure we've got a few good years in here before we pack it in.

HOWIE. Okay with me. But if you change your mind, let me know.

ALVI. How come?

HOWIE. I've got a proposal for you.

ALVI. What kind of proposal?

HOWIE. It's tough to give up a store that's been your whole life. The daily routine. Moving. Resettling.

SAM. That's very true.

HOWIE. Exactly. It's a big move. So if you decide not to renew the lease, I'm willing to give you each fifty thousand bucks.

ALVI. Fifty thousand bucks?

HOWIE. To ease the transition.

SAM. That's a lot of dough.

HOWIE. You'd be giving up a lot by leaving. And I'd stand to make a lot when you left. So fair's fair.

ALVI. I know what you're up to, Howie. You're trying to ease us out and I'm not biting.

HOWIE. Who's trying to ease you out?

ALVI. You are.

HOWIE. Come on, Alvi. Sign the lease and the place is yours. I'm just trying to help.

ALVI. We don't need any help from you.

HOWIE. Fine. I was just offering.

SAM. I appreciate it, Howie.

ALVI. Well, I don't. If you want to know, we've got big plans for this place. We're going to renovate. Top to bottom.

HOWIE. You are? You're serious?

ALVI. What's so surprising about that?

HOWIE. It takes years to see profit from a renovation. You know that, don't you?

ALVI. Do we know that, Sammy?

SAM. We know that, Howie. But we've been here forty years. A couple more won't make much difference.

HOWIE. You're going to need computers, interfacing, impact studies.

ALVI. We don't need that stuff. I've got everything we need right here in my head. All you young guys want to do is sweep everything old away like it was garbage. I won't be swept away, understand?

HOWIE. Nobody's trying to sweep you away. I just want to make sure you know what you're doing.

ALVI. I know what I'm doing. I'm staying where I belong. Look around this store, Howie. The only place in this whole world where I feel comfortable is when I'm behind this counter with my ledger books open, coffee cups on the floor and the ashtrays overflowing. (*Pause.*) See the nick on this counter? October 12, 1956. Frenchie Dugan slammed it with a bat. He was pissed cause Larsen pitched a perfect game against the Dodgers. I can remember a hundred moments like that. Every cigar burn on the counter was a day in my life. Every coffee stain on the cash register means something to me. I'm not giving this up. Not even for fifty thousand bucks and a condo on the beach. (*ALVI storms off into the storeroom.*)

HOWIE. (*Calls after him.*) Fine, Alvi. I'm not here to argue. (*Pause.*) Sign or don't sign. But I need a decision by tomorrow. (*Pause. HOWIE, frustrated, turns to go.*)

SAM. I'm sorry, Howie. Alvi's a little mixed up these days.

HOWIE. I'll say.

SAM. He's been like that ever since he heard the rent was going up.

HOWIE. He's been like that ever since I've known him.

SAM. It's been worse lately. Alvi's got what they call a type-A personality. There was an article about it in the *Science Times* a couple months ago. He needs everything in order. If things go out of line, he gets frustrated, becomes confrontational, blows up big, then he calms down.

HOWIE. When he calms down, I hope you can convince him I'm not out to get him. I want it to work for you guys. Whatever you do.

SAM. I know you do, Howie. And I appreciate it. More cappuccino?

HOWIE. No, Sam. One's my limit. After that, I got the jitters all day. (*Pause.*) I'm glad we have a minute alone. We never get to talk the way we used to. (*HE takes off his jacket, loosens his tie, sits down.*) You doing okay?

SAM. I'm doing fine. Keeping busy. Staying in shape. Would you believe, only eighteen more credits and I'm a college graduate. Psychology major, with a minor in Physical Education. Not bad for an old guy from the neighborhood. Huh, Howie?

HOWIE. Not bad at all, Sam. Bernice would be proud if she could see you.

SAM. I wish more than anything she could be there when I pick up my diploma. Her eyes would be running with tears to see her Sammy walking down that aisle.

HOWIE. I loved Bernice, Sam. I get choked up still when I talk about her.

SAM. She loved you too, Howie. Of all the kids who came in the store, you were her favorite. She always said, that Howie, he's special. He's going places. And she was right. Look at you. Big, successful real estate developer, power breakfasts, car phones, franchises. Quite a life you're living.

HOWIE. It's okay.

SAM. Just okay, Howie? That's discouraging to hear. Makes you lose faith in *New York* magazine.

HOWIE. You want to know the truth, Sam?

SAM. I wouldn't mind.

HOWIE. Buying and selling and redeveloping. It's what I do and it makes me money, but it's not really what I love.

SAM. What do you mean? You got an MBA and a car phone. You were groomed to take over the business.

HOWIE. I did that to make my father happy. But ever since I was a kid, there's been one thing I wanted to do more than anything else. One thing I've never had the guts to try. And now, Sam, I feel like I'm too old and have too many responsibilities to do it.

SAM. What's that, Howie?

HOWIE. You'll laugh at me if I tell you.

SAM. I won't. I won't. I promise.

HOWIE. You know me. From the time I was a kid I've been making up jokes, writing them down, going over them in my head. (*Pause.*) A couple of years ago, I realized that what I really loved doing had nothing to do with buildings and rents and real estate. What I really want to be, what I've always dreamed of being, is a stand-up comic.

SAM. A stand-up comic?

HOWIE. It sounds crazy, I know. But that's what I want to be. More than anything. Just to stand on a stage in a spotlight making people laugh ...

SAM. (*Pause.*) Isn't that strange.

HOWIE. What?

SAM. There was an article just last month in *Self* magazine. They said every person has another person deep inside. Dying to get out. But things hold them back—fears, doubts, age, responsibilities. Sometimes, this article said, we try so hard to keep the hidden person down, that it never gets a chance to breathe. And when that happens, the hidden person kind of suffocates, slowly, day by day. And when finally that hidden person dies, it's like a piece of us dies too. Our hopes. Our souls. I'm not making this up, Howie. It was all there. In the April issue.

(*Pause.*) If I were you, I wouldn't let that hidden person die.

HOWIE. You wouldn't?

SAM. No. I'd do what I wanted to do. Before it was too late.

HOWIE. You would?

SAM. I would. You want things to change? You have to change them. Stick your neck out, don't worry about looking like a fool.

HOWIE. I wouldn't know where to start.

SAM. I tell you what. There's a guy named Monte Berg. Runs the Laffs Club in Paramus. An old customer. Been coming in for years. (*Goes to Rolodex behind counter, pulls out a card.*) I'll call him up if you like. Ask him to listen to you.

HOWIE. You'd do that for me?

SAM. Of course I would. We dreamers have to stick together. You have material?

HOWIE. Are you kidding? I've got forty minutes. Impressions, songs, everything.

SAM. Let him hear it. Who knows? Maybe he'll put you on amateur night. Then I can say I knew you when you were nothing but my rich landlord.

HOWIE. He'd give me a shot?

SAM. All the free gloves I gave him? It's the least he could do.

HOWIE. You don't know what this means to me, Sam. I've never told anyone about this. They'd say I was crazy to try.

SAM. You're not crazy, Howie. You're fighting the good fight. Keeping your dreams alive. It's good to know there's a comic inside of you. I thought you were nothing but numbers and deals. (*Pause.*) I'll call this afternoon. Tell you what he says. But you have to do me one favor in return.

HOWIE. Whatever you say. It's yours.

SAM. Promise you won't be rough on little Zachy. Even if he make fifty errors he's a good boy. And he tries hard. Don't make him feel like a nothing.

HOWIE. Okay, Sam. I just wish he was a little more coordinated. (*Pause.*) I'm going to cancel all my appointments for today and go home and rehearse. (*Picks up jacket and briefcase.*) Thanks, Sam. For everything. (*HOWIE exits.*)

(*SAM is alone a moment when ALVI returns.*)

ALVI. The snotnose gone?

SAM. If you mean Howie, yeah.

ALVI. Can you believe that kid? Trying to bribe us out of our store.

SAM. He wasn't trying to bribe us.

ALVI. A lot you know, Sammy. That snotnose was pretending to be our friend so he could ease us out. And you fell for it.

SAM. He wasn't pretending. He *is* our friend.

ALVI. He's our landlord. Sammy. A landlord is not a friend.

SAM. Howie's different.

ALVI. He's not different. He's a snotnose like the rest of them. (*Pause.*) Yesterday, I'm walking through my building lobby when this snotnose urologist from the fourth floor comes up to me. His kid has a new baseball glove and the urologist says to me, "Hey, jockstrap. Do you sell these at your store?" Jockstrap he calls me, Sammy, this urologist. What do I tell him? I tell him I'd rather play with jockstraps than play with piss and putzes. And if he talks to me again like that, I'll wrap him three times around the flagpole. Urologist or no urologist.

SAM. Think what you want, Alvi. We're just lucky he didn't change his mind about giving us a lease the way you carried on in here.

ALVI. I carried on?

SAM. Yeah. You carried on.

ALVI. Look, Sammy. I know something about business. He's after something.

SAM. You think you know everything, Alvi. But you don't

ALVI. You know more, I suppose?

SAM. What would you say if I told you Howie doesn't even want to be a landlord?

ALVI. He's a landlord. You can't stop being who you are.

SAM. He may be one now, but he just told me that deep down in his truest heart he doesn't want to be a landlord at all. Never has.

ALVI. What does he want to be?

SAM. A stand-up comic.

ALVI. (*Pause.*) A stand-up comic?

SAM. Ever since he was a kid.

ALVI. Howie Golden never told a good joke in his life.

SAM. That doesn't matter.

ALVI. Of course it matters. How can he be a stand-up comic if he can't tell a good joke?

SAM. What matters is that he wants to do it. Now he has the chance. I'm getting him an audition with Monte Berg.

ALVI. Monte Berg knows talent. He'll say he's terrible.

SAM. Maybe he will, maybe he won't. He'll never know until he tries.

ALVI. (*Pause. Puzzled.*) What kind of world is this, Sammy? Where everyone wants to be someone else?

SAM. People just want to find out who they are.

ALVI. What for? You reach a certain age, you don't have time to be other people. You barely have time to be yourself. People should be more like me. I know who I am. I don't need to fool around being someone else.

SAM. And you know exactly who you are?

ALVI. What you see is what you get.

SAM. Come on, Alvi. I've got eyes. I can see.

ALVI. What do you see?

SAM. I see the way you look at yourself in the mirror when you think no one's watching. Like you did in the old days.

ALVI. What does that prove?

SAM. Nothing. It just tells me that underneath that exterior of yours there's an other whole person. The guy I knew when we first started. The sharpest dresser ever to hit Roseland. A guy with guts, and verve and style.

ALVI. You talking about me?

SAM. Yeah, Alvi. I'm talking about you.

ALVI. (*Long pause.*) You really think, after all these years, I've got guts and verve and style?

SAM. It's still there.

ALVI. You're not kidding me, are you Sammy?

SAM. No way, Alvi. I mean every word.

ALVI. Stay right there. Don't make a move.

SAM. Where you going?

ALVI. Stay there and don't ask questions. I'll be right back.

(*ALVI rushes off to the storeroom. SAM checks his watch, looks in the mirror and does a couple of mambo steps. Walks to door. Turns the "closed" sign around to read "open."*)

SAM. Hey, Alvi. What are you doing?

ALVI. (*From offstage.*) You'll see.

SAM. Come on, Alvi. This is no time for games.

ALVI. (*From offstage.*) Hold your hat, Sammy. I'll be right there.

SAM. (*Remembering.*) Hey, Alvi. Remember that night at Roseland when you proposed to Harriet. Right up on the bandstand.

ALVI. (*Returns excited from the storeroom wearing an elaborate jogging suit.*) Okay, Sammy. Behold.

SAM. Will you look at that.

ALVI. The Nike Wind Runner. Satin outside. Cotton lined. Velcro sleeves and ankles. Every morning this week I'd come in early, put it on and walk around the store. And you know what, Sammy? For a few minutes, instead of feeling like an old man, I felt like the guy I used to be. Trim. Athletic. Not bad to look at either. (*Pause.*) Then, when I knew you were coming, I'd hang it away in the back because I thought you'd say I looked dumb. (*Pause.*) Tell me straight, Sammy. Do I look stupid in this thing?

SAM. No, Alvi. You look terrific.

ALVI. You're not just saying that?

SAM. No way. Blue's your best color. Goes perfect with your eyes.

ALVI. I've got another secret.

SAM. This is a big day for secrets.

ALVI. There's something magical about this suit. Something that makes certain things happen.

SAM. What kinds of things?

ALVI. Six o'clock this morning I took my shower, splashed on some Old Spice and got ready for work. Before I left, I figured I try on the Wind Runner and see what Harriet thinks. So, I slip it on, run a brush through my hair, and tip-toe quiet into the bedroom to kiss Harriet good-bye. I bend over the bed, like I've done a million mornings before, but this time, instead of sleeping, Harriet's looking up at me. No, Sammy. Not looking. She's gazing like a young girl. And then ... you're not going to believe this, Sammy.

SAM. I 'll believe it. What happened?

ALVI. She pulled me into the sack.

SAM. No kidding?

ALVI. And ... I cut the mustard. At six in the morning on a working day! (*Pause.*) Suddenly, I thought, if this could happen from a Wind Runner, I've been missing out on some pretty good things. I ordered a dozen more this morning. I'll wear a different one every day of the week. Who knows what could happen then? Who can tell? (*Does a little mambo step.*) Hey. You didn't tell me. How'd you make out in the mambo contest?

SAM. I don't want to talk about it.

ALVI. What do you mean? You won, right?

SAM. No. I didn't win. I came in second. Behind Murray the Drycleaner.

ALVI. It was fixed. He bought off the judges with free alterations.

SAM. It wasn't fixed. I didn't have it. No kick. No bump. No nothing. I imagined everything, just like you told me, and then I stepped all over Angela's feet.

ALVI. A fluke. That's what it was.

SAM. It was no fluke. The magic's gone. Last night, while I was dancing, I caught a look at myself in the mirror. I expected to see a twenty-year old kid out there on the floor. Instead, I see an old man.

ALVI. You had a bad night.

SAM. No, Alvi. I'm getting too old to mambo. Maybe too old for other things too.

ALVI. Like what?

SAM. Like starting over again in the store.

ALVI. What did you say?

SAM. I've been thinking, Alvi. Maybe we should take the fifty thousand like Howie said and forget the renovation.

ALVI. Forget the renovation? Are you nuts? I did the numbers. I ordered Wind Runners. I turned my life upside down and now you're backing out for a lousy fifty thousand?

SAM. I'm not backing out.

ALVI. What are you doing then?

SAM. I'm worried it won't work.

ALVI. You got me into this, Sammy.

SAM. I know I did.

ALVI. You can't back out on me now. I need you.

SAM. (*Surprised.*) You do?

ALVI. Of course I do. I can't renovate alone. We renovate together or we don't renovate at all.

SAM. You mean that?

ALVI. Yeah. I mean it.

SAM. What if it doesn't work?

ALVI. We'll make it work.

SAM. But what if it doesn't?

ALVI. Then we'll go down. But we'll go down fighting. Like partners. (*Pause.*) I want to tell you something, Sammy. This life is funny, you know? You work with a guy forty years, side-by-side. You share things with him you'd never share with anyone else. But at the same time, you take him for granted, stop listening, start building up little angers and resentments. (*Pause.*) Then, one day, you retire or they raise the rent and you realize that all those years went by and you never told him how you feel about him. Really feel. Deep down inside. So I want to tell you now, Sammy. Before it's too late. I love you. I just want you to know that.

SAM. I love you, too, Alvi. Whoever you are.

ALVI. (*Pause.*) So? Are you in or out?

SAM. I'm in, Alvi. I'm scared. But I'm in.

ALVI. Then there's only one thing left to do.

SAM. What's that?

ALVI. Let's sign the lease and drink from the fountain of youth. (*HE takes pen from counter and signs the lease.*) To Alvi and Sam. Partners to the end.

(ALVI hands pen to SAM. HE signs.)

SAM. To Sam and Alvi. The undisputed over-age kings of sporting goods. Don't worry about me, Alvi. I don't want to take over the books and the ordering. I just want to talk and sell the goods. Like I've always done.

ALVI. Then it's a perfect match. A fast pencil and a big mouth. How can we lose with a combination like that? (*Pause.*) Time to celebrate.

We'll order in breakfast. Fried eggs on a hard roll. Coffee black. The works. Then I'll give you another mambo lesson. Next time, you'll wipe the floor with Murray the Drycleaner. Guaranteed.

SAM. I don't know, Alvi. I feel like a fool dancing the mambo.

ALVI. No, Sammy. A fool's the guy who stops dancing. Not the guy who dances on. (*Pause.*) I'll put on music. Some nice Tito Puente to get you in the mood. (*HE puts on a tape. MUSIC plays. HE comes back and opens his arms.*) Come on, Sammy. It's time to mambo! Remember, Sammy. It's all in the rhythm and it all comes back.

(*SAM and ALVI dance an inspired mambo as the MUSIC continues and the LIGHTS slowly fade to black.*)

THE END

COSTUME PLOT

SAM: Act I
Pale teal green Lacoste shirt
Deep teal green sueded zip jacket jogging suit.
  "Elysse" brand.
White athletic socks
White sneakers or running shoes
Walkman in pocket with head phones
(Removes jacket in Act I)

Act II
Light brownish-grey "Sans-a-Belt" trousers
Brown slip-on shoes
Brown socks
Navy blue, long-sleeved Dior sport shirt with
  epaulets (open at neck)
White V-neck T shirt

ALVI: Act I
White T shirt
Plaid, short sleeved, button-down sports shirt
Khaki unpleated pants
Beige socks
Brown loafers
Mets baseball cap

Act II
Blue oxford button-down sports shirt (short -
  sleeved)
Tan pants
Webbed belt

Grey, round neck T shirt
Repeat socks and loafers

Fast change into:

Bright, blue and white "Nike" sweat suit with
  zipper jacket
Repeat grey round neck T shirt
(add white sneakers using white elastic laces for
  quick change)

HOWIE: Act I

White, round-neck T shirt
Modern, abstract "Sergio Tachini" expensive,
multi-colored jogging suit
White athletic socks
White, expensive "status" sneakers
Gucci or Louis Vuitton narrow leather briefcase
Diamond pinkie ring
Diamond "Rolex" Watch, gold band
Gold neck chain
Sunglasses—Cartier type

Act II

Blue, "Sea Isle" 100% cotton long-sleeved shirt
Yellow Foulard "Power Tie"
Tan summer suit, three button. Pleated trousers
Belt—tan with status buckle
Pocket square
Brown socks
Brown Gucci-type loafers
Repeat, watch, ring, briefcase.

PROPERTY PLOT

<u>SAM - Preset offstage</u>
brown paper bag w/ 2 containers of coffee, 2
   danish (cheese & prune), sugar, knife, napkins
newspaper and magazine
Walkman w/headset

<u>ALVI - w/costume</u>
pen (blue top, silver bottom)

<u>HOWIE - w/costumes</u>
briefcase w/leases
wallet w/photograph of kid

<u>Main counter</u>
towel
rack of sweatbands, baseballs, pins
magazines
cash register
pads of paper
container of pens, etc.
adding machine
<u>rear counter, shelves, walls - all SR</u>
2 stools
baseball cap
telephone
radio
phone book and Rolodex
memo board
container of pens, etc., paper
baseballs

trophies
chest protectors
clinchers (softballs)
batting tees
football helmets
Spaldings (rubber balls)
Gary Carters -7 (catchers' gloves)
catchers' mask - 7 small, 8 medium
shin guards - 8
<u>file cabinet</u>
check book
2 books w/inventory
file w/leases
<u>upstage</u>
rack of clothing
trash barrel
a few boxes
<u>upstage shelves</u>
basketballs
shoulder pads
footballs
tennis balls and racquet
<u>SL Wall</u>
shoes on display
baseball bats
shoe boxes
one shoe box opened with shoe laced
pile of newspapers on floor
boxes
free standing mirror
baseball gloves
golf clubs

3 chairs - attached and footstool
<u>Intermission</u>
set bag w/croissant, coffee, napkins on counter
set 1 croissant on napkin
strike shoulder pad to make room
move football helmets to upstage shelf
set table DS left w/rack of sweatbands, baseballs,
    etc.
set Walkman on table
turn around adding machine

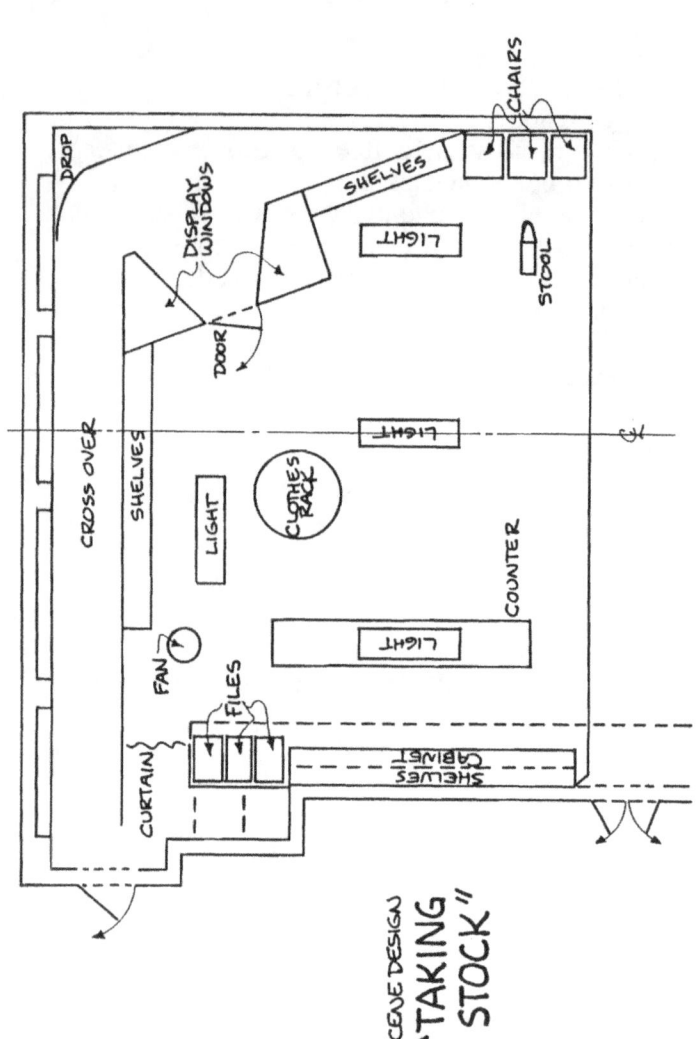

SCENE DESIGN
"TAKING
STOCK"